A Gutterful Life

A Gutterful Life

KAPIL RAJ

Anecdote
Publishing House

Anecdote Publishing House
E-35-A, E Block, Gali No. 2, Ganesh Nagar,
Pandav Nagar Complex, Delhi - 110092

Published by Anecdote Publishing House
Copyright © Kapil Raj

First Edition 2023

ISBN: 9788195890712

MRP: ₹ 149.00

Book Promoted and Marketed by Champ Readers Pvt. Ltd.

Layout and Cover by Anecdote
Printed in India

To all the free souls,
hurt, chained, and caged
by social rules and
fabrications.

Change Stories by

Kapil Raj

Change Stories by Kapil Raj is an amalgamation of five independent short stories: ***Kuroopa, A Gutterful Life, First Love Many Times, Flying with Chains, and A Mother By The Window.***

Advancement of humankind invariably poses new challenges to the existing social order in society. It weakens the bondages enforced by patriarchal rules, paving the way for societal awakening. However, every ounce of progress leaves behind some debris in its wake. Failure to recognise this debris or 'problem' can bestow acute misery and suffering in the lives of people. Going back and snipping the problem in the bud is usually more cumbersome than revolting and moving forward.

If only there was an easy way out.

> *True social development cannot be achieved without breaking existing stereotypes and adapting our mindsets to the subsequent changes.*

Each short story interweaves a heartening story with a deeply imbibed social issue, hardened public belief, and associated fabrications. As you read the narrative, you watch and evolve with the characters, sometimes feeling yourself in them – empathising in circumstances that may or may not have existed in your lives. The stories will highlight the suffering that was never supposed to take place had we brought about a meaningful change for ourselves and others in the society.

However, there's always a first, and it can start here.

> *We live how we think, and we think how we choose to live.*
> *Progress is hard; change is heroic.*

Acknowledgements

Every beginning has a story. We often emphasise too much on the journey and the end goal, forgetting all about that *first step*.

When I commenced writing *ENDURER A Rape Story*, I was scared spending nights on the outcome. From the inception of the idea to getting the story published, three years passed. The book finally, reached the hands of readers and found love in a way I had never imagined.

For the first time, when I held the mic in a room full of young students to speak on the subject (rape and sexual assaults) which is considered one of the biggest taboo in the Indian households, my hands trembled, yet I took that leap.

By the end of each of session, I was gifted emotions, witnessed appreciation and respect. It was a dream come true. But a thought lingered behind. What next? What topic should I pick? Will I be able to justify the appreciation and recognition I received? The turmoil was too much. For a moment, I felt giving up. In those times, there are people who stand with you, influencing in ways which do not let yourself stop and take on unfamiliar paths.

They are my parents, my wife Payal, my sister Dimple and my son Hetarth. I owe you.

Pulkit, Thank You. You always stood along. When I simply could not progress further, your faith in me made me hold on and continue to move.

Tatiana, I am grateful for your persuasion and astute conversations. You incepted ideas on which I was able to write and build these stories.

Tina, you have my gratitude. You chiselled out the entire work with your editing and added a clear voice to the words.

Sincere thanks to Anecdote Publishers & Sagar Azad, who trusted me with my unconventional project and extended all support to get published.

And most importantly, I would like to thank all my readers. Your reviews, personal texts, praises and critiques motivated me to walk through this journey.

1

Aklaq and Somu met on the bridge over the neighbourhood naala for the first time. Somu ran back and forth with a pinwheel in his hand. The breeze made the pinwheel go faster, despite the stink of filth it carried. The faster the wheel rotated, the happier Somu became. All his efforts to clean the bench for Chai Chachu had paid off.

Somu would clean the bench of the tiny tea stall close to his house and throw all the leftover plastic cups in the sewer for a few days, and in return, he would get this toy to play with. The pinwheel lasted a few days before getting lost or torn. Somu would believe he misplaced it, but his older brothers would steal it for playing and rip it while they frolicked. Somu would continue to work, hoping to get a new toy to replace the one he had lost.

As Somu ran across the bridge, his excitement knew no bounds. He thought he was a superhero flying across the canyon to save the world, aided by his powerful machine. He wasn't sure what needed to be saved in the world, but he would do it anyway. He jumped, sat down, and had a few laughs. He toyed with the pinwheel in different ways, enjoying the joy this simple contaction brought him.

Another boy of comparable age watched his game. They both looked similar – dusty, torn shirts, ragged bottoms, no slippers, unkempt hair but, with one difference – the boy who looked on had a small webbed cap on his head. Somu could see the longing in this boy's eyes. He also wanted to play with the fan and fly in the wind.

Somu went up to him and asked, "Want to join?"

The boy nodded instantly. Somu gave him the pinwheel, and the boy started jiggling the fan in the air.

"No, no, it will break if you do this," exclaimed Somu, taking it back. "This is what you need to do," he said, holding the fan and suddenly shrieking, "Run!". Both the boys flew across the *naala* with no holds barred, momentarily leaving their hardships behind and making their way to discover a new world. They continued to play through the afternoon without caring for food or water. No one looked for them or called them back home. The fewer mouths to feed, the better, but their bodies finally gave in.

"Come," said Aklaq, taking Somu across the bridge to his side of the *naala*. This was a first for Somu. He had never crossed to the other side. There was frequent talk about Hindu families and Muslim families, but he never much understood the difference. Amma had once told him to stay on their side of the *naala*. That is when he had heard the term "Muslim" for the first time.

"Amma, who are we then?"

"Hindu," responded Amma, while rubbing some utensils with *rakh* for cleaning.

"Who made us Hindu?"

"Bhagwan Ji," she replied.

"The one who lives in the temple?"

"Yes, yes!" she replied, laughing at his innocence.

"And who made Muslims?"

Amma glanced at Somu and continued to work, avoiding the question. She did not give him an answer, but the query remained in his mind.

The muddy street looked similar on this side of the *naala*, so did the crossing lanes and the houses. Women were washing utensils and clothes, their buckets clustered under communal taps. They stopped in front of a crumbling house, the top two floors seemed to be hanging on precariously. When they entered the house, Somu found an open area with two huge wooden carts. Aklaq ran and hugged his father, who had just returned home from work.

He lifted Aklaq in his arms and handed him a stale orange.

"Abba! I wanted an apple. You promised."

"Next time Akku. Apples are very costly these days. Even the stale ones get sold."

"Abba, this is Somu, my new friend."

Aklaq's father gave an orange to Somu, too. The boys happily grabbed their gifts and ran back to the bridge. Each slice of the fruit felt tangy and sweet to the tongue. Somu did not remember the last time he had an orange.

"Does your papa have a lot of money?" asked Somu.

"Why?"

Somu gestured towards the orange. Fruits were a luxury. They had to be satisfied with vegetables, roti or rice at their house.

"No, no. My Abba sells fruits. The stale ones get reserved for us. I often wonder what fresh ones taste like."

Somu nodded and devoured the last piece. They continued to play with the pinwheel. After a while, they invented a new game – who could throw the orange peels the farthest in the *naala*.

2

Aklaq's fruits and Somu's toy provided meaning to their newfound relationship. Somu worked hard to get his pinwheel, and Aklaq helped his father pick up and select the fruits, keeping an additional one for Somu. They played, narrated stories, shared their dreams, and often sat by the *naala* late into the evenings to watch the sunset. The fading orange light of the setting sun shimmered over the murky water flowing below. Refuse such as polythene bags of different colours, broken bottles, pieces of cloth, things that have lost their identity, all submitted to the gloom of the *naala*. But in that moment, right before giving up, it was their final chance at glory, when the beautiful dim light fell over them, to discern how they felt when they were alive – to know they had some purpose. Because after death, nothing remains except darkness.

"Have you ever been to the city, Aklaq?"

"Not yet."

"I wonder if they also have this *naala*."

"Ammi says they are bad people. They live a good life but send their filth here to us. Allah would punish them, somehow."

"Who is Allah?"

"The one who created this world, Somu. If we

pray to him and follow his path, all our wishes will come true."

"Amma says the same about Shiva. He lives there –" said Somu, pointing at a temple that looked tiny from where they were sitting.

"You have many Gods, but we believe in one, Allah. We pray to him."

"Hmmm. Let us pray that we get these many toffees one day," said Somu, stretching his arms wide.

"And we finish them together in one day."

They laughed, and they prayed. It is believed that God hears a child's prayer quickly, as their hearts are pure. In the case of Somu and Aklaq, either their wish was rejected, or there was nobody to listen to them.

#

One individual drinking water pipeline ran on both sides of the *naala*, connecting to a few taps. Even a small deviation from the water schedule would cause chaos, so everyone made sure to fill their buckets every morning and evening. However, one day, the pipeline on one side got damaged due to some maintenance work around the *naala*. Filthy, unclean water was usual, but the channel completely broke this time. The people on the "broken" side had no option but to utilise the tap on the other side for immediate use. The community elders rushed to the local authorities to get the issue resolved. This unfortunate incident created immense chaos for everyone – long queues formed before the taps while people waited to wash their wares. The last time this happened, it took about three days to fix the pipeline.

Some men left for the neighbouring settlements early in the morning to fetch water. The elders clustered near the pipeline to run interference if someone cheated or a fight broke out. It was a big responsibility on their frail shoulders. People think becoming old makes you stubborn and senile, unable to reason or understand. On the contrary, age brings a multitude of experiences gained through years of struggle and turmoil. This experience enables them to make rational decisions. As young individuals, we don't act but react in a unidirectional outburst, which is precisely what Billu did when he kicked Arif's utensil out of the line.

"I'm saying this for the last time; his dirty pot should not touch my bucket!" screamed Billu.

The elders left their chairs and tried to resolve the conflict. People rushed to see what the commotion was all about. Few attempted to break the fight, some were enjoying the show, while many others were egging the two parties on, trying to make matters worse. It was the last category that was the most despicable.

"So, you think you can come to our side and kick our utensils? How about we charge you for each of your buckets?" screamed somebody from the crowd.

"Charge? Chacha, this tap does not belong to anyone. It is public property!"

"Oh, it does. This is our side."

3

Billu and Arif had a history together. Billu sold momos outside a girl's college on the highway. He was the only hawker on the entire street next to the college gate, which gave him a monopoly. Students would flock around him throughout the day – lunch hours were busiest. He would get sold out every single day, making a lot of profit along the way. A recently acquired second-hand television became the talk of the community. One day he was having tea at Chai

Chachu's stall when Arif crossed his path. They started to talk and discussed their professions. Billu boasted about his farsightedness and how he milked the opportunity for all its worth. Onlookers, along with Arif, praised his tenacity. When the college was off for summer vacations, Billu decided to take a break and went to visit his ancestral village. Unfortunately, flooding of the nearby river derailed his plans and he could not come back when the college reopened.

Billu was frustrated about missing two weeks of earning. However, when he finally made it back, he reached the college to find Arif standing under the tree with a momo stall. Anger flared inside his heart and he wanted to strike Arif then and there, but the considerable flock of students stopped him in his tracks.

"You backstabber!" he yelled when the crowd had thinned and almost all students were back inside for their classes.

"This is no one's place. We all have mouths to feed," replied Arif with a smile.

"This was my area," said Billu, grabbing Arif's collar.

Arif extricated himself and gently placed his hands on Billu's shoulders in an incredibly polite and natural manner.

"Calm down, brother: your area, your customers. I am simply standing on a side. Your stall is still there, right next to the college gate. We can share, can't we?"

Billu stomped away and waited for the lunch hour. He reminded himself that his customers would remember him and that Arif's presence would make no difference. However, customers are like free birds who belong to no one. As soon as the recess started, most students flocked towards Arif's stall while a few stayed loyal to their original vendor. Billu was left bewildered, unable to understand Arif's magic trick. Most of his stock remained unsold that day.

For the first time, he was returning home with meagre earnings. The fading daylight made Arif's tiny board shimmer, and Billu could read the reason why Arif was more popular. He was selling chicken momos in addition to the vegetarian option. Billu stopped packing his things and sat down, contemplating what had just happened while Arif left happily. Until now, he was worried about his absence – thinking that maybe Arif's momos were tastier and his secret recipe was better. But if the hurdle was a choice between vegetarian and non-vegetarian, he would never be able to get over it. It wasn't just about being a vegetarian himself. Billu was the only son of the temple priest. Consuming meat is a controversial subject in Hindu families. It is mostly frowned upon, yet many Hindus partake by choice. Whatever the global consensus on this topic is, Billu will never be able to sell chicken momos, that much was for sure. Father is a priest, and the son sells non-vegetarian food? No! It was not going to happen.

His inability to do anything further substantiated his hatred. Muddled by betrayal, Billu instead channelled his anger towards Arif and his community.

"So why did you throw his vessel? Is he untouchable?" Arif's friend quipped in jest.

Untouchability based on the caste system is a sensitive topic. It is still prevalent in some cities, the concept has a more profound practice in smaller towns and villages. This abhorrent practice had surpassed several impediments and roots in many rural communities' mindsets. The problem lies in human nature striving for pride and power, while beliefs are just placeholders to toy with. A typical brain finds this hard to comprehend, and hence the masses suffer from discrimination without understanding the history, logic or origin of this stigma. Most people take its advantage insensitively, which is what Arif's friends were doing – trying to enrage Billu and coerce him into committing a folly on a public platform. People lived by the *naala* due to their circumstances and not by choice. They were the lowest ones on the ladder, with the worst living conditions. Already shunned by the people in the city, this discrimination within the community dwellers was quite an igniting factor.

"You want me to speak up, do you?" said Billu, still furious.

"Yes, tell everyone. Why did you throw the bucket?"

Billu fumed in silence. He did not want to say anything, but these people left him with no choice. Some of them were trying to break the fight and convince Billu to leave, but the exploiting ones had overtaken the skirmish.

"He must explain his actions."

"Because he is filthy on the inside and outside. This water is for the temple and will not be spoiled by the touch of a meat-eater. He was doing this on purpose, and I will throw his bucket again if needed."

4

Words lose their meaning. Truth is nothing but a troublemaker. Everyone asks for it; nobody wants to hear, accept, or acknowledge it. During simpler times, the cause of a confrontation was either truth or lies. There was no middle ground. As time passed, we understood the impossibility of living with just these two concepts, giving birth to new ones – half-truths, diplomacy or truth without context. These concepts have more viability and are backed by some pretty good reasoning. Individually, both truth and lies can be quite bland, but mixing them up gives rise to innumerable theories and speculations. Situations can be twisted and turned into deception – in the end, they tend to be more useful in making people mould their opinions.

Billu was dragged away; a group separated Arif and his aides. The elders requested the impetuous and opinionated members to not fall for the kids' arrogance, but to no avail. After the crowd dispersed, a few people remained at the *naala*, watching the queue and feeling nostalgic about old times. They had spent their entire lives scurrying around that giant, ever-flowing gutter. The *naala* was their hope, the dividing line, and it was for good – they needed it. Without its existence, the neighbouring communities would have fought and destroyed themselves long ago. No one spoke about it, but being divided this way united them. Whatever they did during the daytime, in the end, they all came back and lived peacefully with each other within a safe, known distance. Because, more than fighting for religion, caste, or community, they had a much bigger adversary to defeat – poverty. Only a morsel of food can calm a toddler's howling after hours of hunger. Nothing else works!

There had been conflicts before and resolved as well. But every time, the conclusion was the same. The guiding force behind the verdict was never mental acumen, but the realisation that fighting hurts everyone. God or religion are never the cause of a fight; the lack of their understanding is. To be honest, more than faith, it's personal motive that drives the skirmishes.

History has no significance, as it can be twisted to suit the present. As the next day dawned, work on the pipeline resumed and people sighed with relief. But Billu's altercation continued to make rounds. On both sides of the *naala*, people only focused on their version of the truth. On one side, they thought that Arif took advantage of Billu's absence, took over his business, and was mocking him by deliberately shoving his bucket to touch Billu's. Arif knew the water was for the temple and how sensitive Hindus were about cleanliness, particularly about their places of worship.

On the other side it was being discussed that opportunities wait for no one. Feeding their family is everyone's birthright or moral responsibility. If not Arif, somebody else could have arrived and given competition to Billu – religion had got nothing to do with this. Billu had no right to throw Arif's bucket into the *naala*. He had insulted the entire community by calling Arif a meat-eater and declaring their wares were impure to touch. Does this imply that all Muslims are tainted who follow the guidance of the scripture? This was sheer disrespect and deserved an apology.

The power of half-truths.

5

Gopi followed his passion for cars. Unlike other boys involved in profitable occupations like puncture repair, *halwai*, men's salons, etc., Gopi cleaned cars in a posh society in the city. He would admire them as living beings at different stages of life, having diverse builds and strengths. His hands wouldn't stop unless he saw his face reflected in the beast's body. He compensated for his low wage by working at an ironing stall for the rest of the day.

Watching his younger brother Somu working at a tea stall, Gopi finally agreed to grant him his one wish – a ride to the city. He foresaw that Somu could join him in a few months so they could cover more cars. Despite Gopi's constant tirade of warnings and precautions, Somu and Aklaq could not keep their excitement at bay. On the next day, Somu wore his best shirt and shorts with the least number of holes.

With Gopi's permission, Somu sat on the rod in front of the cycle's seat and Aklaq positioned himself on the back stand. Their excitement lacquered over any pain that they experienced when the cycle hobbled over rocks or potholes. The moment they crossed the edge of the *naala*, Somu's heart started to flutter. He turned slightly to look at the boundary from where their home began. It was a new beginning, a fresh chapter unfolding in Somu and Aklaq's lives, and they were embracing it with glee.

The cycle flew across the interconnecting lanes
of the suburbs and soon hit the city's main road.
Hundreds of vehicles honked simultaneously,
trying to overtake each other and find a way out
when there was none. So many autos, rickshaws,
scooters, bikes, and cars of different designs
were on the way to their destinations. All along
the road there was a smattering of shops selling
oddities like jewellery, clothes, eatables, etc. – all
strange and unfamiliar things to the duo. Somu
wondered how people with such fair complexion
stood without moving, wearing such fancy clothes
and accessories behind the showroom's glass
windows.

This was the real world; this was the destination.
The kids were stunned and amazed at the view.
They had never even seen the things locked inside
Chai Chachu's containers, let alone this. A box
of light played a strange game on the road. It
changed colour in short bursts of time. Everyone
would rush, slow down, or stop on a specific

colour. Somu liked the transition from green to red the most. This is when the people exerted all their might to cross, as if it was a matter of life and death. He did not appreciate his brother and other cyclists who cheated and did not stop at those lights when others did.

Soon the cycle turned towards a colony lined with exquisite homes and numerous cars. It seemed they had reached their destination. Aklaq calculated a few car spaces equalling their homes. The scent of the flowing *naala* was missing, there was no dust, and everything seemed to reflect colours – the walls of the houses, the lustre of the road, the greenery all around them. Only the sky felt familiar because that is where Allah stayed and watched us, Aklaq thought.

"Dada, why can't we live here?" asked Somu as they parked their cycle near a stall – a bigger version of the one Chai Chachu had.

Gopi looked at the lady who managed the stall and laughed at his brother's innocent question.

"Picnic?" asked the middle-aged lady.

Gopi nodded. The lady opened a drawer and pulled out a tennis ball. She offered it to Somu. Astonished, Somu looked at Gopi.

"Didi, I don't have the money to pay..."

"Don't worry. This is a gift for these little monkeys."

Gopi nodded and smiled. Somu stepped forward gingerly, a little shy to take the gift.

"Don't think I am being kind. There is a tiny dent on this, but you can play with it," she said, pointing to the garden in front. "Go there. I'll watch over them while you work."

Gopi warned the boys not to make excessive noise and be careless. He also told them not to speak to anyone. In any case, he would be back in an hour or two and by then they would have finished playing.

The lush green park greeted the duo with a cool breeze, just like a gateway to heaven. To their left was a series of swings and slides. One glance at each other, and they bolted towards them as if the rides would disappear if not caught in time. They jumped, fell, slid, bumped into each other, and rolled on the soft grass like there was no tomorrow. Continuing their feat, Somu threw the ball in the air and Aklaq reciprocated by trying to catch it despite the slippery mud. After a couple of hours, Aklaq paused for a while and handed over a guava to Somu. They lay down on the grass and watched the sky, relishing every bite.

"Today is the best day of my life," said Somu, brushing his hand over the earth.

"Mine too."

"I wish when we grow up, we could come here and play like this every day."

"I don't know. When we grow up, we will have to work and support our family," said Aklaq with a bit of sadness.

"Don't worry, we will take a break once a week. Plus, there is still time for us to grow up. How old are you?"

"I don't know."

"So you don't know when your birthday is?"

"No. Ammi says we shouldn't celebrate birthdays, so she doesn't reveal any of our dates."

"Hmmm. Mine is two days after Holi."

"That colour festival?"

"Yes. I love birthdays. We will celebrate together this time."

They giggled and continued to play until Gopi returned to take them back to reality.

6

It is doubtful if people ever desire peace. If we sift through history carefully, we will find that peace is just a pause between acts of violence. In the name of commitment, leaders propagate personal motives laced with pride and greed for power. Their followers believe and accept the lies that are fed to them, directly or through social conditioning. Eventually, the situation leads to different interests, perspectives, and conflicts. Every country has a similar story.

We yearn for peace only when we are fed up with violence and its associated tragedies. Slowly and steadily, as the period of stillness grows longer, a sense of boredom sets in and we are back to our old ways – deliberate situations are created for battles and skirmishes. I do agree that we all want to live in harmony, but somehow we also crave unsavoury circumstances for personal entertainment and excitement. Peace is like one of the seasons. And by the *naala*, this season was on its way out.

The incident between Billu and Arif created a wave of resentment, unearthing bygones and older memories. It also brought to light one of the biggest hypocrisies one can notice within our social structures. In this world, each individual is different, has a unique understanding of their principles and moral code of conduct, and reacts to circumstances based on the knowledge gained through personal experiences. Giving a generalised verdict only because the person lives in a particular region, with a particular community, or belongs to a specific religion is quite insane and unintelligent. Unfortunately, this concept has not only gained roots in our mindsets, but it has found a way into legal systems too.

Everybody waited with bated breath for the political spectacle to unfurl at the *naala*. Word was spread to disrupt any efforts to bring back the peace. Billu's story got twisted with each retelling, causing well-established cross-*naala* relationships to crack. If one had to repair a fan, they would visit an electrician on their side of the *naala* only. If not available, they would wait instead of getting it repaired right away by the available electrician on the other side. Noticing this behaviour, other people followed suit. Instead of questioning the immoral practices, people preferred to follow the herd. Groceries, vegetables, hair salons, repairs, everything became 'Us against Them' – unity in division.

Chai Chachu was in a unique position. He lived on one side of the *naala* and was the only one who had to cross the boundary to earn a living – his stall was on the other side. The younger generation had forgotten Chai Chachu's story, but it was quite something.

Chachu's actual name is Hasan. Bear with me before you make assumptions after learning his name. The *naala* broke off diagonally from the main city road, flowing for a kilometre, and then concluding in a river. The constant combat between the heavy outflow and small opening often caused overflow at the beginning of the *naala*. So every day, with the help of sticks, some people would pick up the litter clogging the outflow and throw it aside. This had resulted in a heap of garbage, that was only growing larger with every passing year. In addition to the plastic, cleaners found unthinkable things in the dried-up pile – nail polish bottles, eyeless dolls, wooden necklaces, scraps, but had never found anything as outrageous as a human child. They would find a mutilated corpse once in a while, but a baby's cry was quite unexpected.

The child was alive – it was a miracle! Which caste did he belong to? What was his religion? Which God or angel protected him? Nobody knew; no one cared. But his fair complexion and brown hair indicated that he belonged to an upper-class family. The honourable families that throw infants in the garbage to rot and be eaten alive.

The news spread across the *naala*, and the child was brought to Kumar's tea stall. This is where most of the community dwellers thronged for their morning tea, read newspapers, and discussed politics. Yes, Chai Chachu currently owns it.

"Mia Rashid, I have a good feeling about this kid. I am going to keep him," said Kumar as he played with him. Kumar and Rashid had been friends for life.

"You already have four kids. I am one short. Let me take him and we will be even," replied Rashid. The listeners laughed. There was a time when people believed that more boys meant additional helping hands.

Rashid took the boy in his arms and said, "So beautiful. We will call him Hasan. May the miracle of his birth bring some luck to our communities." Rashid died after a few years in an accident, as we were told. But everyone knew that he had been caught in the middle of a fight between his helping hands, and to protect them from each other, he suffered a blow and fell from the window. Hasan was just five years old when he witnessed this horrific incident. Rashid's death resulted in petty squabbles over each morsel of food. His sons kicked Hasan out of the house right away – additional hands also meant an extra mouth to feed, a luxury they could not afford anymore.

Devastated by his friend's demise, Kumar accepted

Hasan with open arms. Rashid had a soft corner for Hasan right from the beginning; maybe he foresaw his boys' conduct so was overprotective for his adopted child. The tragedy swept away Hasan's innocent understanding of love and filled him with the fear of losing everything. He started suppressing all his emotions, because sooner or later, nothing would last. His brothers accepted his request to sleep beside Ammi, as long as he didn't ask for food. So Hasan toiled the entire day, working endlessly and only returning home at night.

Kumar's heart would bleed watching Hasan work so strenuously. In him, he saw Rashid. Kumar had offered him a place to stay, but Hasan had refused. He did not know where he belonged anymore. His brothers had divulged that he was found in the garbage. Lost and disillusioned, he continued to work in silence, without a smile or expression – only his eyes revealed the pain inside him. The Imam would frequently scold youngsters to offer their prayers properly, but with Hasan he would talk gently, consoling him by telling the prophet's stories. The priest in the adjoining temple narrated the stories of Hindu deities, watching a boy kill his childhood without a word. Who knew what was in his heart? Who was his keeper? Who was his God? Was he a Hindu or a Muslim?

Before dying, Kumar distributed his stalls in the city amongst his sons, but he kept the favourite one for Hasan. His roots, his soul remained where he grew up, where he endured the ups and downs of life, met Rashid, spent days and nights solving community problems, and finally passed from this world. The *naala* was just a sewer to an outsider, but for Kumar, it was his world, his paradise. He knew his soul would always linger around there. Hasan accepted his new responsibility silently. The stall, which was like a courtroom a few years ago, where people discussed issues, resolved conflicts, noted women's complaints, and acted upon them, was no longer the same. Those people were gone, and so was the sentiment. Gone were the days when people came out of their houses to chit-chat after sun down. The city's discarded electronics found life there after repairs. Radios, TVs, and phones replaced human conversations.

We say the world is connected; Hasan never felt that way. If the connection has nothing to do with feelings, it is as good as not having any. Emotions make or break the world; the rest is an illusion. All this technological drama of social connections is making people self-contained and lonely. Hasan never reacted, but he had observed the people, taking care of each other and being genuinely interested in resolving conflicts. Things were different now. No one noticed his eyes, understood him, or wanted to talk. He existed and yet remained non-existent. The end was near, but something prickled inside him to witness a lost emotion. With age, we forget our feelings. But life experiences have a tendency to trigger the memories long lost or forgotten.

7

Billu was mocked whenever he crossed Arif
or his friends. Even in the crowd, there would
be an unmistakable grin or scornful look, and if
alone, there was no end to the ridicule. One of the
boys would question the status of the business, or
initiate excessive touching while others pushed
Arif around, yelling that he had not taken a bath and
was filthy, mocking Billu's public outburst. Billu
remembered his father's words and contained his
anger – he refused to get riled up. But with every

passing day, the bullying became worse, and it became harder for Billu to keep his emotions in check.

One fine evening before the Holi festival, the tyre of Billu's cart punctured when coming back home. The nearest shop on the street was closed, but he could see the mechanic lying drunk in the backyard. Billu took the tools from his shop and repaired the cart himself with whatever limited knowledge he had. A lot of time was lost, and he got late for the ceremony at the temple.

The fire near the temple shone from a distance. Billu was still hoping to make it to the festivities in time. When he crossed the garbage dump and entered the lane, a few boys started walking alongside him.

"Oh, momo brother. How was your sale today? Got your spot or still lingering around?" One of them touched the cart and ran away.

"Hey, what have you done? Now his cart has become impure," said another, laughing his guts out.

Billu's fist tightened, and his jaw stiffened.

"Listen, today is our festival. Do not spoil my mood, Arif, or else..."

"Else what?" said Arif, his voice emanating from the shadows.

"You dare insult us, instructing which is our side?"

"Yes, and right now, you are not on your side. Run away before I thrash you with my slipper," said Billu, bending low to take off his slipper.

A boy pushed him from behind and Billu toppled over, landing at Arif's feet.

"You think very highly of yourself, don't you?"

said Arif, punching Billu in the chest. He was surprisingly strong for such a lanky person. Billu slipped and fell in the *naala*.

The world abides by many unsaid laws; there was one for the people living by the *naala* as well – whatever happens, do not fall into the sewer. The impurity, neglect, discard, and truth of human nature flowed through this gutter. Living beside it was a constraint. Many people had left this place behind after creating a better life elsewhere, like Hasan's brothers. Many others continued to stay, working hard to get out of the stink one day. They were born into it, so were compelled to accept the humiliating conditions – whether by choice or by force, it did not matter.

The boys fled; they didn't turn even once. Arif knew they had made a grave mistake; this had gone too far. His instructions were to heckle and incite Billu to commit a similar mistake again, not to humiliate him beyond repair. Standing alone, he wanted to help, pick Billu and apologise for his behaviour. But there was a time for everything, and it had passed. People nearby heard Billu's screams and rushed towards the scene.

With some help, he finally managed to walk out, drenched head to toe in the murkiness of the gutter, shame burning his insides. He walked through the lane slowly and reached the temple. Unstoppable tears gushed out of his eyes as the body quaked with anger and disgust. The rejoicing paused, all eyes swelled with shock when they realised that the dark, walking figure was Billu. Children screamed at him; his own mother howled after watching her son's condition.

Panditji emerged with a bucket of water and splashed it across his body. After several buckets, Billu tore the clothes off his body and threw them aside, discarding his fate with them. His face reddened with a deepening darkness.

"Who did it?" asked someone. Everyone knew the answer.

Billu looked up and pointed his finger towards the other side of the *naala*.

"Go home like cowards and sleep, but I won't!" he yelled.

People circled him – few in anger and many in shame. The priest locked the temple and stood beside his son, muttering mantras and sprinkling Ganga water to purify his soul.

"This is wrong; they should be held accountable!" said one of them.

"Wrong? This is a crime, Pappu. They pushed my son into the filth of this city. It's an act that has never been committed in the history of the *naala*; none of us have witnessed it!" yelled Panditji.

"Day by day, their nuisances are increasing."

"Block the bridge," said somebody.

"Is that even possible?"

"I won't unlock the temple until someone is penalised for this crime. How long can we keep getting tortured like this for? I'm sure those kids are being provoked by their elders."

"Let us be reasonable, Panditji. Generations have lived in harmony beside the *naala*. I am calling Imam Sahib. They will send those boys and make them apologise to Billu in front of us. If not, then we'll see what needs to be done. We will take some action for sure. The kids are getting swayed by politics."

As it turned out, no one came forward to apologise. Arif accepted his mistake, but his so called friends ditched him and refused to relent.

They even threatened him and said there would be consequences if he snitched on them. They could behave this way because they had enough support from certain individuals in the community who considered themselves superior. Some of the elders tried to reason with the influential members, but who listens to peacemakers these days? Remember, peace is just like one of the seasons – it comes and goes with convenience.

Billu slept on a bench outside the temple in the open; he did not enter his house. The temple remained locked. The last call was finally disconnected, all warnings in vain. There was no cheer during the festival of Holi this time. There was only anger, fear, and worry all around. The community elders were anxious about the consequence of their decision, but they realised it had to be done because the message had to get out. A group of men were gathered who created a temporary wooden barricade around the bridge. The news travelled quickly; the opportunists made calls. The community leaders requested the police to stay away from their business. It was as if the water had not boiled enough. Blood! That's what they were after. There had to be some bloodshed before the sharks dived in and further messed up the lives of simple people in return for the obvious – a flourishing vote bank. The message reached the concerned parties on both sides. Boil the sentiments leading in breakage of the barricade resulting in a deadly fight.

8

For a few days, Chai Chachu had no idea of his surroundings. His body ached and was wracked with fever. Hasan had never been absent from work for a single day in his entire life. Whatever be the case, he would walk up to his stall and work. His neighbour's daughter was quite kind and would ply him with food and medication. Despite being told to rest, Hasan left his house to go to work that day. It was mid-afternoon. He was worried about being late. His ability to open the shop on time was getting impacted with age and time. Another concern was the absence of a family – he did not have a wife or a child to pass his business to. A few people were preying on his shop, but no one dared to ask openly.

As he walked towards the bridge, Hasan saw a wooden barricade and a few people sitting behind it. The crowd exchanged looks when they saw him approach.

"Billu beta, what is all this?"

"Chachu, this path has been blocked. Ask your egoistic community members."

"But I have to open my shop, beta."

"Forget it, Chachu. We tried our best, but no one listened. This is how it is now."

Hasan stared at the motley group that was blocking his way. Billu, today a tall, sturdy boy, who used to play on his lap and pull at his beard all the time. Next to him sat Manoj, who still owed Hasan the money he had borrowed when police officers thrashed his vegetable stall and his relatives refused to help. Sushil, Lokesh, Hari, they all had a deep-rooted history with Hasan. They would run naked, playing around the temple and the stall. Today they were obstructing the path to his shop. Each one of them had shared memorable moments at the stall; what had got into them today?

Hasan sat on the edge of the bridge to rest his feet and watched the debris floating along the *naala*. At a distance, Aklaq sat with his head bowed; sadness lacquered all over his face. Hasan noticed a toy in his hand, a wooden cart with wheels, and a small handle to drag it by. On realising he had been noticed, Aklaq shifted and hid the toy behind his back.

"Why aren't you playing?"

"This is for Somu. Today is his birthday. These people are not letting me cross."

Hasan's heart started thumping, all weariness fading away. He kissed Aklaq on his forehead and asked him to wait. Then he chatted with one of the elders present there and got a gist of the entire story. His rage elevated with every passing word. After Hasan had heard enough, he stomped off the bridge as if leaving for war. He reached Arif's house and yelled out his name.

Many people had forgotten what Hasan looked like when he was angry, but when Arif saw him, he was taken aback. A tall, broad-chested old man with blazing eyes and flowing hair – he looked like an angry angel sent by the almighty Allah. The moment Arif came out, Hasan grabbed him by the ear.

"Hasan Mia, what are you doing?" screamed Arif's father.

"Doing your work," replied Hasan, dragging Arif by the ear in front of everyone.

A few spectators stood up and tried to block their path. One of them had called Imam Sahib, who rushed towards the scene. He was in charge of the "bridge barricade" plan. A sizable donation for the mosque and the *madrasa* was promised in exchange for prolonging the feud.

"Hasan, leave him!" screamed Imam Sahib.

Hasan looked around for the source of the sound – he was surrounded by numerous men by now. The women watched from the balconies and roofs of their houses.

"You are no one to decide for all of us. Those people have initiated this divide, and we will reply like true Muslims!" screamed Imam Sahab, publicly.

This announcement was greeted by silence, and everyone went still. A smile splayed across Hasan's face. Witnessing it was a first for most people present there. Hasan closed his eyes and raised his palms to the air.

"Wa-ʿtaṣimū   bi-ḥabli   llāhi   jamīʿan   Wa-lā tafarraqū."

Hasan's voice pitched differently while he uttered these words. The crowd was stunned – a recitation from the holy Quran, with such fluency and rhythm, was usually heard from the mouths of speakers or Imams, not regular people. Moreover, no one had ever seen Hasan visit a mosque like other devout Muslims.

Hasan turned around, and explained.

"Hold fast, all together, to Allah's cord, and do not be divided."

"Oh! So you can recite verses from the Quran. Then do not commit sin by misinterpreting the meaning in front of innocent people. The words hold true only for Muslims," said Imam Sahib.

"And who are you to decide that? We are all Allah's servants. If anyone has the right to punish us, it is Allah. You want to divide this place forever over a senseless scuffle between a few youngsters? Where are your efforts to resolve this conflict? Since when did the elders become so careless? Does our entire life here mean nothing, that two boys can just prance about and decide the fate of everyone? Imam Sahib, shame on you. I am taking this boy; he will apologise, and so will Billu. If anyone tries to stop me, they will have to go over my dead body."

Hasan pushed through the crowd and walked out, dragging Arif behind him. The onlookers just stood there, gaping at each other. The indecisiveness was fading; there is nothing more beautiful than determination and true intent. As Hasan stepped on the bridge with Arif, people near the barricade stood up from their vantage points. Few of them rushed back to call for more support.

"Remove this right now!" screamed Hasan.

The men looked at him, stupefied. More than the baritone of the commanding voice directed at them, they were astonished by the figure calling them out while dragging the culprit by his ear.

"Speak here first," said Ajju, noting the silence.

"Beta Ajju, I will speak to your mother first. She pleaded with me to lend her a hundred rupees so she could pay the nurse that delivered you. I am still waiting to get my money back. Add the interest of 26 years."

Ajju, blinded with shame, turned away. No one had the guts to stand up to Hasan. He stared at everyone for a while, provoking them with his eyes to get a reaction. When nothing happened, he took a deep breath, mustered all his energy, and aimed a kick at the barricade. People watched as the rickety obstruction toppled over along with the chairs by a single strike of an old man.

Hasan let go of Arif's ear for a while after reaching the stall. He unlocked the stall, lifted the shutter, swept a little, and placed the desks in the open as usual.

"Sit, both of you!" ordered Hasan, pointing at Arif and Billu.

Arif obeyed and sat on the bench. Hari poked

Billu on the shoulder and asked him to follow. Billu accepted unwillingly and sat beside his rival. "Arif!" said Hasan, his unwavering stare piercing the boy's soul, instructing him to do the right thing.

"I apologise, Billu," said Arif with his head bowed. "Yes, I took advantage of your absence to establish my business. But I didn't know it would affect you in such a big way because you had your customers. I had no realisation of the non-vegetarian angle until you got back. Do you think only Muslims love my chicken momos?"

Arif raised his eyes now.

"I am not as expressive as you are, and your behaviour has hurt my feelings. My mischief and taunts were just my way of stating my frustration. The pot throwing incident – I had never thought you would brand my entire community as untouchable."

"And lastly, I am sorry for taking this episode so far – I had no intention of pushing you into the *naala*. There is no excuse for this and definitely it turned into an unfortunate event."

Everyone, including the Imam Sahib and the community members from the other side, heard Arif's confession.

"Billu!"

Billu glanced at Chai Chachu with surprise. He wasn't aware of anything he had to apologise for. He wasn't in the wrong, Arif was.

"What did I do, Chachu? I reacted only because he stole…"

"No, Billu! You failed to understand that the world is not a place of comfort. Every person struggles in their own way. When we are children, we are

free. But those children are free because there are
adults who take responsibility for their actions,
who takes care of them. And for that, they have
to struggle. If not Arif, there would be another
person competing with you. With him it is better;
he is from your neighbourhood."

Hasan's voice became louder, but a dull rumbling
continued. Away from this hubbub, hidden behind
the throng of people, Aklaq stood with his eyes
fixed on Somu. Oblivious to what the commotion
was about, Somu stared at his friend.

"The poison in your hearts enabled a barrier to
take hold in our community. It's not just Billu, all
of you are responsible. Can you stop breathing
the air that has touched Arif? Can any one of you
divide the sunlight or split the sky? This side, that
side! To the city, we are nothing but a smidge of
dirt. Imagine a barricade separating us from them
one day. How will that make you feel?"

"Come here boy!" Hasan called Somu and made him stand in front of Billu.

"Look into his eyes and tell him he will never see his friend again. A friend from the other side who has been waiting across the barricade for hours to hand him a toy for his birthday."

Noticing Hasan's finger pointing at him, Aklaq walked towards them.

"All of you, tell these boys they have made a mistake. Explain to them why they need to separate."

Billu was overwhelmed with anguish. Yes, he should not have insulted Arif and his entire community. He knew that it wasn't Arif who had pushed him into the *naala* – he had tripped over. We all know the truth behind our mistakes, but our egos make it difficult to accept them. Often, the realisation comes long after any possibility of correction, unless we are lucky and receive an epiphany.

Billu glanced at Aklaq and his sad face.

"Did your Abba buy it?"

"No, I earned the money and purchased it from Baba myself."

Billu was not the only one touched after hearing this. Baba was a known toy maker who sold wooden toys in gatherings and religious places. This boy would have worked very hard to purchase that toy.

Billu looked at the surrounding people – his father, Chai Chachu, and the two boys. He raised his hand and offered it to Arif.

"I apologise too. I should not have behaved

so rashly. I forgot that my actions would have consequences."

Arif responded with a smile. Chai Chachu clapped his hands and started pouring tea into cups. The barricade was dragged away from the bridge. The masterminds behind the destruction watched their plan getting demolished. The crowd scattered; a few rested on the bench.

Somu and Aklaq hugged each other and jumped around, playing with the toy.

"Chachu, two of that orange one," asked Somu, pointing at his favourite candy. As soon as Hasan handed them over, the boys devoured them without delay.

"Come back," said Hasan and gave them two more.

The kids jumped with excitement and ran towards

the bridge. Watching Somu and Aklaq play without a care in the world, Hasan saw his father Rashid and uncle Kumar again. It was as if a gentle breeze enveloped his mind, refreshing his memories – the lost feeling.

Hasan slept that night without a weight over his head. Tears of happiness flowed through his eyes. The body is just a cage; the soul's hunger can only be quenched with noble feelings and emotions. His longingness for this world ended. He was absolutely clueless about where he would go now, as, in this world, the people had segregated skies and heavens. They had decided where they would go after death, despite being utterly clueless about the lives they live. Religions had become mere tools to justify the wrongdoings. No one went back to their scriptures for confirming their noble deeds. And this has been existing for centuries. Hasan had not found God even after reading all the scriptures – nobody knew this. But there existed a flame in every living being, that Rashid and Kumar helped him identify. That fire didn't just burn, but threw light and got bigger with love, humility, and gratitude. And for his part, that flame would pass on to Somu and Aklaq. He had found the heirs to his stall.

Change Stories – Next Reads

Kuroopa

'Why did God make me so ugly? Am I not your daughter? Was I exchanged at the hospital? Or did you leave me in the sun one day and that's why I became so dark?'

Meera, one of three siblings, has been struggling with her identity since childhood. She is subjected to mean, insensitive remarks by neighbours, relatives, and random people around her due to the lack of pleasing physical attributes. Constant comparison with her fair, blue-eyed sister further deteriorates her relationship with friends, family, and most importantly, herself.

A shocking incident involving the household pets pushes Meera over the edge, forcing her parents, especially her father, to take action and bring her back to reality.

Will Meera be able to find her footing in this hypocritical world that preaches "looks don't matter" while constantly objectifying and running towards beautification? Will she be able to accept herself for who she is and overcome the hatred she has for herself?

First Love Many Times

'She is my life; she is my love. What will I do if I fail? True love only happens once in a lifetime.'

Abhi falls head-over-heels in love with Kavya at first sight. They become friends and everything is beautiful as if they were destined to be together. Until the day Abhi confesses his love for her at the Taj Mahal.

Catastrophe befalls and Abhi's dream shatters. Completely heartbroken, Abhi decides to fight for his love one last time, like the ones shown in movies. If successful, life would be beautiful again, else he would have to end his life.

Will Abhi be able to understand the difference between true love and the one displayed on screen? Will he see reason beyond his anguish? Does love truly happen just once?

This short story debates the question about first love and the trials and tribulations one goes through to achieve it.

Flying With Chains

Three friends – Yatin, Taruni, and Kunal – have been joined at the hip since childhood. They live close by, go to the same school, and always hang out at the same rendezvous. As they grow up, their parents become uncomfortable about their closeness and try to keep them apart.

Whether it's Yatin's struggle to clear the civil services examination, Kunal's difficulty in convincing his businessman father to let him pursue physics, or Taruni's rebellion to break free from the shackles of patriarchy, undue expectations from friends and family builds the pressure on this trio.

Will their friendship withstand the test of time or will the demands of society unravel their relationship and lead to mistrust and betrayal? Will they be able to chase their dreams or will they succumb to their inevitable fate?

A Mother By The Window

'A final lesson for her, she thought. A woman's happiness resides outside herself, in places defined by society.'

Neetu, an obedient housewife, devotes all her time and energy to take care of her family. She is diligent and abides by the rules society has laid out for her. Nostalgia of winning a beauty pageant many years ago and regret of marrying early encourages her to try her hand at becoming an influencer on Instagram.

She works hard to achieve her new goal, without disrupting the life she was married into. Her attention eventually gets divided between her dream and family, bringing to light the secret she is harbouring. The secret hurts her image of an "ideal wife" much to her husband's chagrin.

With Neetu's life in turmoil, Rahul takes a stand to save his mother's dream.

Will Neetu realise her true potential and achieve her dream? Are women expected to fulfil only one role at a time, and no other? Does a woman's personal life belong only to her family? Is there any hope for change?

Also by

Kapil Raj

*N*ow, a national bestseller.

Life was a fun fed roller coaster: new found love, drugs, cat-fights, patch ups, crushes, night hangouts, and unplanned trips. Like any girl, not in the wildest dream, palak could imagine that after attending a rave party, she will wake up to the horror of finding herself raped.

In traumatic conditions and struggle between sanity and hallucinations, she is compelled by the circumstances to leave her world. Already fighting a war within, her stances take a toll witnessing horrifying tales of women and girls. Little did she know that this catastrophe was not enough for one lifetime, and a storm — was just cooling its heels.

Will she be able to carve her path while facing the rapists, her tyrant father, appearances of her passed away mother? Should palak let her life to be decided by people, society, and taboos? Would justice return her life or revenge lend her peace?

A heart-rending story of a girl, whose beliefs and honor has been battered, stands up to make choices, rediscovering the meaning of life.

About the Author

$\mathcal{K}$apil Raj is a professional, speaker and writer-activist based in Delhi-NCR, India. With the heart of a philosopher, mind of a realist, and a deep-rooted non-conformist, he lives many lives, yet stealing the time for the most precious thing that matters to him: crafting plots, playing with characters, and weaving the stories based on intricate social subjects and challenging the dogmas.

His debut novel *ENDURER A Rape Story* is critically acclaimed by the media and loved by the readers. He is a noted speaker and delivered lectures in prestigious institutions and colleges.

Connect with him on Facebook, Twitter, Instagram @ikapilraj